⌐ancy Dicks was born in East Ham, London, in 1935. After graduating from Cambridge, he began work in the advertising industry before moving over to television as a writer. In 1968, he began working on *Doctor Who*. He has written over fifty *Doctor Who* novels and has also been a prolific author of books for children.

MADE OF STEEL

Made of Steel

Terrance Dicks

BBC
BOOKS

2 4 6 8 10 9 7 5 3 1

Published in 2007 by BBC Books, an imprint of Ebury Publishing.
Ebury Publishing is a division of the Random House Group Ltd.

The Random House Group Ltd Reg. No. 954009.
Addresses for companies within the Random House Group can be found at
www.randomhouse.co.uk.

A CIP catalogue record for this book is available from the British Library.

ISBN 978 1 846 07204 8

The Random House Group Ltd makes every effort to ensure that the papers
used in our books are made from trees that have been legally sourced from
well-managed credibly certified forests. Our paper procurement policy can
be found at www.randomhouse.co.uk.

Mixed Sources
Product group from well-managed
forests and other controlled sources
www.fsc.org   Cert no. TT-COC-2139
© 1996 Forest Stewardship Council
FSC

Creative Director: Justin Richards
Project Editor: Steve Tribe
Production Controller: Alenka Oblak

Doctor Who is a BBC Wales production for BBC One
Executive Producers: Russell T Davies and Julie Gardner
Producer: Phil Collinson

Cover design by Henry Steadman © BBC 2007
Typeset in Stone Serif
Printed and bound in Great Britain by Bookmarque, Surrey

MADE OF STEEL

CHAPTER ONE
THE RAIDERS

THE MEGATECH CENTRE WAS the first to be hit.

It was the biggest and best computer and electronics store in Britain – possibly in the world. A big modern showroom in the heart of London's West End. Inside, it was all glass and steel, packed with everything from bog-standard PCs to the latest MP3 player. MegaTech advertised everywhere: press, telly, Internet, mailings... *Upgrade today! Limited offer! Lowest prices ever! Buy now!*

And buy they did. Monday to Saturday, 8am till 6pm, customers flooded in, prowling display stands and shelves, grabbing overworked assistants, spending all they could afford and more. Anything to keep their precious computers and electronic gadgets up to date – even though up to date would be out of date by next week.

MegaTech reckoned to cope with any kind of customer. But not the ones who arrived at 3am one morning.

The vast showroom and the storerooms behind were dark and silent by then. Only a few dim lights were working. Old Trevor, retired policeman and senior nightwatchman, sat in his chair by the main door, thermos and sandwiches by his side. Kevin, his assistant, was off somewhere checking the storeroom.

Kevin was keen, so let him get on with it. Trevor knew that MegaTech was protected by the finest alarm system in the world. If anybody so much as breathed hard on any of the outer doors and windows, bells would ring, sirens would howl, lights would flash and linked alarms would go off in the local cop shop.

Technology was there to make a man's life easier. Let it do its job.

Trevor poured strong sweet tea into the cup of his thermos, unwrapped his sandwiches and took a bite of cheese and onion.

Suddenly the air seemed to shimmer in front of him. He took off his glasses and rubbed his eyes. Maybe he'd put off that overdue eye test too long. He replaced his glasses and stared. A circle of light was forming in the centre of the showroom floor...

At its centre appeared a shimmering, metallic figure. Slowly it became solid. The thing was terrifying. It was more or less man-shaped but much bigger than any man. The head carried a sort of crest with strange handle-like attachments, and the face was a terrifyingly blank steel mask. Trevor jumped to his feet, dropping his sandwich and spilling his tea. 'Ere!' he shouted feebly.

The metallic figure raised an arm and a gun barrel clicked into place at its wrist. Energy pulses of scarlet light flashed out, and Trevor staggered back and crumpled to the floor.

A second, identical figure shimmered into existence beside the first.

Ignoring Trevor's body, the steel figures moved out of the circle. They began moving among the display cases. Some they passed by. Others were shattered with a sweeping blow of a powerful metal fist. The contents of some of the cases were carried to the circle of light and stacked inside.

In the storeroom, Kevin heard the sound of shattering glass. Drawing his only weapon, a truncheon, he ran towards the sound.

He stopped in the doorway of the showroom, staring round in disbelief. Trevor's sprawled body. Smashed display cases. Two huge silver shapes moving among them.

The nearest of the giant figures turned and saw him. Kevin turned and ran, and the gleaming figure stretched out a metal arm. Scarlet light pulses flashed again. Kevin spun round and fell. The silver figure strode past him into the storeroom.

Next day, the official police statement spoke of 'a well-organised robbery by a well-equipped and highly professional gang'. Some things were not mentioned or explained. Both showroom and storeroom had been looted of the latest high-tech equipment. Yet the alarm system had failed to go off – even though it was found to be in perfect working order.

The deaths of the two security guards were equally mysterious. No one seemed to know quite what had killed them. The post-mortem revealed only 'a massive shock to the system, caused by a force of unknown origin'.

The second guard, younger and stronger than the first, had still been alive, just, when found. He died in hospital a few hours later, muttering about 'silver giants'. There was no reference to this in the official accounts.

The second attack took place in the heart of Whitehall itself. The secret research lab behind the Ministry of Science, a building so secure that it was often described as a giant safe, was attacked and robbed. Most of the night staff were left dead.

The only survivor, a research assistant, babbled about giant silver figures stalking among the ruins. He was immediately moved to a secure sanatorium.

A search revealed that highly secret equipment was missing, including top-grade surveillance gear and a state-of-the-art decoding machine.

The sign on the heavy metal gate read:

CHADWICK GREEN
HER MAJESTY'S GOVERNMENT
RESEARCH AND DEVELOPMENT CENTRE
Strictly No Admittance Without Pass

It was the small hours of the morning, nearing the end of a cold and damp night. The rain had stopped, replaced by an icy wind. The harsh light of the arc lamps surrounding the camp shone down on the wet parade ground and the huddle of barracks, storerooms and labs on the other side.

The sentry on duty at the main gates was Dexter Hanson. He was tired, bored and fed up. He wanted hot tea and a warm bed, and he wanted to see his girl, who worked in the pub in the village. He suspected she was also seeing Corporal Harris. When he got off duty, Hanson was going to have it out with her.

He glanced at his watch. Only half an hour till he'd be relieved. He decided on a bit of a stamp to warm himself up and vent his frustration and anger.

As he swung round to begin his march, Hanson saw a giant silver figure, already *inside* the gates. It was stalking towards the row of lab buildings on the other side of the parade ground.

For a moment, Hanson stared in disbelief. Then he yelled, 'You there! Halt or I fire!'

The figure whirled round, raising an arm in a pointing gesture. Hanson was a combat veteran – he'd seen action in both Iraq and Afghanistan. He reacted instinctively, hurling himself aside to the ground. The energy blast missed.

Springing to one knee, Hanson raised his automatic rifle and fired shot after shot into the silver figure.

It ignored the attack and fired again. Dexter Hanson screamed, twisted in agony and fell lifeless to the ground.

The shots had alerted the camp, and a shirt-sleeved corporal ran out of the guardhouse, blazing away with an automatic pistol. The silver giant fired at once, blasting him down.

A second silver figure appeared beside the first, and the two began to march towards the rows of buildings.

A general alarm blared out, and armed men began to emerge from all sides. The silver giants were hit by a hail of bullets, but the weapons had no effect. One by one, the soldiers were ruthlessly shot down.

An armoured car sped towards the intruders. It had a heavy mounted machine gun, which was pumping out bullets. Both metal figures fired at once, and the vehicle exploded in flames. They resumed their march.

They reached the door of the nearest lab building and effortlessly smashed it open...

CHAPTER TWO

FIELD TRIP

'STEADY NOW,' SAID THE Doctor. 'Take it slowly. It's a timid creature. It's probably more frightened of you than you are of it. Really.' He grinned. 'No offence.'

'None taken. And who's frightened?' said Martha defiantly. 'I mean, it's only a flipping great prehistoric monster the size of a house!'

She nervously held up the bunch of juicy green palm fronds to the giant creature towering above her.

Martha Jones was the Doctor's current companion. A medical student, she had met the Doctor when terrifying alien forces had invaded the hospital where she was training. When it was all over, she had accepted his offer of 'just one trip'. Somehow that one trip had become the first of many.

Now they were standing outside the TARDIS at the edge of a clearing in the middle of a lush prehistoric jungle. The air was hot and steamy, filled with the cries of strange, and no doubt savage, creatures.

The Doctor had fished out a battered bugle-like object and had used it to produce a weird high-pitched sound.

'Works like a duck-call,' he explained. 'Though on a slightly larger scale, obviously. Appeals to animals slightly larger than ducks too. Which is useful – because there aren't any ducks yet. Here we go!'

And, sure enough, an enormous creature had lumbered out of the jungle towards them. It had stumpy legs, a vast bulky body and a tiny head on the end of an incredibly long neck.

Suddenly the tiny head snaked down and snatched the palm fronds from Martha's hand.

Martha looked up the dinosaur as it munched away high above her.

'You're sure it won't want *me* for afters?'

'Oh, you'll be all right,' the Doctor assured her. 'It's an Apatosaurus – strictly vegetarian. Well, almost strictly.' He paused to consider. 'Or nearly almost. Perhaps it's vegetarians it eats. Now if I'd called up a Pterodactyl, or even better a T-Rex...'

As he spoke, Martha felt the ground shake beneath her feet. A huge shadow fell over them. The Apatosaurus gave a shrill scream of terror, wheeled round and lumbered away with surprising speed.

But Martha wasn't watching. She and the Doctor both turned to see the enormous creature behind them. It was so tall that its head was blotting out the sun. A massive, brutal shape, silhouetted against the sky.

'Did I say "even better"?' the Doctor wondered out loud. 'Might not have meant that exactly.'

As the monstrous head dipped rapidly towards them, the Doctor grabbed Martha's hand and dragged her inside the TARDIS. The creature's sharp, jagged teeth clashed on the empty space where Martha had been standing a moment before. Seconds later, the TARDIS faded away. The Tyrannosaurus's mighty jaws again snapped shut on empty space.

Or almost empty.

On the spot where the TARDIS had vanished, the air shimmered. A square shape began to form...

Safely back inside the TARDIS, the Doctor said, 'Sorry about that. Maybe we'd better stick to watching David Attenborough in future. Though I don't think he did dinosaurs. Not that close up anyway. So,' he went on brightly, 'where to now?'

'I think I've had enough excitement for one day,' Martha told him. 'Somewhere peaceful. Home. No, not home, that's never peaceful.' She thought again. 'How about work? Hospital,' Martha went on. 'The good old Royal Hope. I'd like to see how everyone's doing. Last time I was there the place got kidnapped.'

'Been there, done that,' the Doctor said. 'Kidnapped hospital? No problem. Soon sorted. Hold on tight then – here we go!'

11

CHAPTER THREE

CRISIS CONFERENCE

THE RESEARCH CENTRE AT Chadwick Green seemed to be back to normal. The Army copes well with emergencies. Wrecked huts and buildings had been removed and rebuilt, and smashed or stolen equipment had been replaced.

A huge team of Army engineers, working day and night, had dug a new security vault. A vast underground chamber with steel and concrete walls, it was designed to protect top-secret equipment from any future attack.

Human problems had been tackled with equal speed and efficiency. Dead soldiers, scientists and research assistants had all been replaced. The families of those killed in the raid were given the Army's deepest sympathy, and fictional reports of training accidents and scientific disasters hid the truth. There were few details – for security reasons, of course. Relatives of all casualties were offered generous compensation, in return for silence and no fuss.

Near the entrance to the vault was the Security Section. This housed a communications centre – air-conditioned, brightly lit and packed with all the latest equipment.

Major Tom Burton, chief security officer, and his number two, Captain Sheila Sarandon, sat before a giant screen, gloomily watching, for what seemed like the hundredth time, grainy black and white CCTV footage of giant silver figures stalking among shattered display cases – the attack on the MegaTech Centre.

They made an oddly contrasting pair. Burton was a massive figure with strong, rather brutal features. His looks weren't improved by a squashed ear and a flattened nose. In his younger days, he'd both boxed and played rugby for the Army. He looked heavy, dull and rather stupid. But, in Tom Burton's case, looks were misleading. 'A rugby thug with a brain like Einstein,' his commanding general had once called him.

Sheila Sarandon was younger and slimmer, a severely beautiful blonde. She was equally bright and fiercely ambitious. The Army was still largely a man's world. She knew that, to succeed, she had to be not just as good as, but better than, her fellow officers.

Tom Burton was well aware that she was

after his job. Not that it worried him. The way he felt at the moment, she was welcome to it. He switched off the projector, stood up, and stretched. 'Doesn't tell us much, does it?'

'It tells us the same as the Ministry footage and our own stuff, sir,' said Sheila. 'The Cybermen are back.'

'I thought they were all wiped out.'

'To be honest, our record isn't too brilliant when it comes to Cybermen,' said Sheila Sarandon scathingly. 'The Cybermen actually had a hidden base *inside* the old Torchwood Tower on Canary Wharf before the big invasion. And there was a breakout sometime after the battle – vital alien equipment was stolen—'

'Including advanced spying equipment and something believed to be an alien teleportation device,' said Burton irritably. 'And now all this. More advanced equipment stolen – from MegaTech, the Science Ministry and here. What we don't know is *why*. What are they up to?'

'They're planning some operation,' said Sheila. 'Something big. Another invasion perhaps.'

'With only two of them?'

'Two's all we've seen – so far. There may be a whole army hidden somewhere.'

'There's a cheerful thought,' said Burton gloomily.

'Got to face facts, sir,' Sheila went on. 'I'm wondering if we should come clean, warn the public...?'

Burton shook his head. 'Out of the question. The invasion and the final battle are too recent. Any hint of it happening again, there'd be nationwide panic – *worldwide* panic. We've got to contain the story.'

'We can't keep the lid on this forever.'

'We can hold it down for a while longer.' Burton slapped a pile of folders onto his desk. 'The relatives of the casualties are squared away, the press and TV under strict embargo.'

'Can't stop gossip and rumour, sir,' said Sheila obstinately. 'There are already scare stories out on the Internet.'

'Just a wacky bunch of conspiracy nuts,' said Burton. 'Nobody's going to pay any attention to them. We've got to keep things quiet till we know what's really going on. The raid on this camp makes it a Military Intelligence problem, Captain Sarandon, and it will be sorted by Military Intelligence – by *us*!'

Sheila Sarandon thought of the old joke about Military Intelligence being a contradiction in terms, but she was too well disciplined to say it out loud.

Burton picked up a folder from his desk. It

was marked 'Top Secret'. 'According to the official reports,' he told her, 'the whole thing was cleared up by this character codenamed the Doctor – the one who apparently works out of an old blue police box.'

'Maybe we should put out an alert for him,' said Sheila. 'Ask the cops to keep a lookout for an ancient police box and a skinny bloke in a pinstriped suit.'

She'd said it as a joke, but Burton seemed to take the suggestion seriously.

'That's not a bad idea, Sheila. Get on to it right away. The way things are at the moment, anything's worth a try.'

She looked at him to see if he was winding her up, and decided he wasn't.

'Very good, sir,' she said, and picked up the phone.

CHAPTER FOUR

HOMEWARD BOUND

MARTHA JONES PACED AROUND the TARDIS console, glancing occasionally at the Doctor as he studied a row of dials and read-outs. Now that her return to the Royal Hope was approaching, she was feeling strangely nervous. How would her old friends feel about seeing her again? How would she feel about them?

'How much longer, Doctor?'

He answered without looking up. 'Oh, any minute now. I should think. Probably.'

'Shouldn't you be steering or something?'

'You reckon?' He frowned, and the frown became a teasing grin. 'No need for that. I pre-set the course coordinates.'

'Yes, but where for? Ancient Rome? World War Five?'

'Oh Martha, Martha, Martha.' He ran round the console and clapped his hands on her shoulders. 'Have a bit of faith. Have a bit of confidence. We may have had the occasional blip. The *very* occasional blip. Or burp. Or hiccup.' He thrust his hands into his trouser pockets and kicked his feet as if embarrassed. Then he hiccupped, making her laugh out loud.

'And, all right, there *was* that unlucky business with Mount Vesuvius,' he went on. 'But be fair. By and large, the TARDIS is pretty reliable these days. Only had to use the hammer twice in the last few trips. I'm even thinking of fixing the chameleon circuit.' He was nodding excitedly, as if to prove this was true. 'The only trouble is, when the circuit was working, I could never find the thing again. I mean, if you can't remember what the TARDIS has changed *into*...' He was back at the console now, staring down at the same set of dials.

Martha had no idea what he was on about. She decided not to ask and changed the subject.

'What's so fascinating about those dials anyway?'

The Doctor straightened up. 'Oh, goodness knows. Do you know? I don't know. Though I started picking up some strange readings as soon as we reached your sector of space-time.'

'What kind of readings?'

'All sorts of stuff. Energy spikes, transmit signatures, Radio 5 Live. Maybe someone's using a teleportation device.'

'A how much?'

'Or a digital radio.'

'At last – something I do understand.'

'Or cellular dissemination.'

Martha shook her head. 'Nope, gone again.'

'Matter transmission – the instant movement of objects from place to place. Well, I say objects – could be people. Even buildings. Like a hospital. Bit of a clue there, did you spot that?'

'Yeah, got that thanks. So what about it?'

'For starters, it's impossible,' said the Doctor sternly. 'At least it ought to be. The technology hasn't been invented in your time.'

'Maybe someone's invented it,' suggested Martha. 'Some mad scientist. Again.'

'Unlikely.' The Doctor frowned. 'But there might be a more worrying explanation.'

'Such as?'

'Someone's using alien technology. Possibly,' he decided, 'an alien. They sort of go together, I find.'

'Oh no,' said Martha. 'Not another invasion. What this time – giant hippos? Intelligent wildebeest? Alien llama maybe? Not more of those ghastly metal men. I couldn't go through all that again.'

The Doctor smiled reassuringly. 'Don't worry. Whatever it is, it isn't Cybermen. The Cybermen were all sucked into the Void. Doubt if it's llamas either, actually.'

'Maybe they got out again. The Cybermen.'

'Impossible. The gap into the Void is sealed, sealed forever. It can never be reopened. Never.' The Doctor's smile faded and, just for a moment, he looked incredibly sad. 'If it could be...'

'What? What's the matter, Doctor?'

Before the Doctor could reply, the TARDIS console gave a series of discreet pings.

'We've arrived,' said the Doctor brightly. 'Show time.' He touched the door controls and peered cautiously outside.

'Well, it doesn't look much like the Circus Maximus in Ancient Rome,' Martha decided. 'And nobody seems to be shooting at us.'

Martha followed the Doctor out of the TARDIS and looked around. A stretch of windswept tarmac, rows and rows of cars, everything from consultants' Rolls Royces to medical students' old bangers. A big white building in the distance.

Martha gave the Doctor an impulsive hug. 'Oh well done, Doctor, spot on. Royal Hope Hospital car park.'

'Of course,' said the Doctor modestly. 'Where else?'

Behind his back, he uncrossed his fingers.

'Come on then,' said Martha eagerly. 'I'll introduce you to all my mates.'

The Doctor shook his head. 'Better not. Some of them might remember me. Best to avoid any awkward questions.'

'And how do I do that?'

'Oh, I don't think you'll have too much trouble. When people are faced with the unbelievable, they tend to react by not believing it. Even when they've seen it with their own eyes. You're a funny lot, you humans.'

'So what are you going to do?'

'I'll have a wander round and get the feel of things. Meet you back here in a couple of hours. Enjoy your reunion.' He gave her a quick smile and strode away in the direction of the busy streets.

'Hey,' Martha called after him. 'Pay and display – make sure you get a ticket or they'll...' She broke off, and looked at the TARDIS parked neatly between two cars. 'They'll wheel-clamp you,' she murmured.

Martha watched in disappointment as the Doctor walked off into the distance. She'd been looking forward to showing him off to all her friends. Still, that was the Doctor for you – hard to pin down. Just when you thought you were best mates, he wandered off.

Perhaps it wasn't really all that surprising if the Doctor sometimes acted unexpectedly. Most of the time, he looked so much like a skinny geek that it was hard to remember that he was an incredibly ancient alien.

Better make the best of it. She headed towards the hospital.

Some time later, a young police constable began patrolling the car park. There had been several cases of theft from cars, even a late-night mugging, and the hospital authorities had insisted that *Something Must Be Done*. PC Jim Wilkie was that *Something*.

He was a keen young officer, just out of his probation period, and he took his job very seriously. Unlike some of his colleagues, he studied and memorised all official messages and orders. Today, for instance, there'd been a strange request to keep an eye out for an old, wooden police box.

PC Wilkie stopped abruptly halfway along a row of parked cars.

'Gordon Bennett,' he thought. 'There it is!'

A blue wooden box. And, to prove it, over the door, were the words 'Police Box'. A notice on the door read:

POLICE TELEPHONE
FREE
FOR USE OF
PUBLIC
ADVICE & ASSISTANCE
OBTAINABLE IMMEDIATELY
OFFICER & CARS
RESPOND TO ALL CALLS
PULL TO OPEN

'Those were the days,' thought PC Wilkie. He tapped the personal radio in his breast pocket. 'Imagine having to find a blue box before you could call for back-up.'

He pulled at the door of the police box but it refused to budge. 'Can't expect it to be still in service,' thought Wilkie.

He called the station on his radio. 'Sarge, you know that call to look out for an old police box. You won't believe this but I've just spotted it, in the Royal Hope car park...' He walked slowly all round the box, squeezing past the cars. 'And it hasn't got a ticket.'

The desk sergeant sighed, put down his mug of tea and noted down Wilkie's report. 'Well spotted son, I'll pass it on. Keep an eye on the box.'

Wilkie's voice crackled out of the intercom. 'What for, Sarge?'

'In case someone drives it away!'

The desk sergeant picked up the phone, called Central Intelligence Clearing, where the request had come from, and relayed Wilkie's report. They'd pass it on to whoever was interested.

'Weird business,' he thought. 'Maybe someone pinched it from a museum.'

He took another swig of tea.

CHAPTER FIVE

CYBERMEN

In a vast, shadowy dome, a tall, silver figure stood over a complex muddle of electronic equipment. Crates holding more equipment were stacked all around.

Nearby, a second enormous figure worked on a smaller installation with a large monitor screen at its centre. A network of cables fed the equipment with power routed from the London Electricity Grid.

A third figure, the Cyberleader, supervised the work of the other two.

'The work goes slowly.' The Cyberleader's voice was harsh, metallic, with a strange fluting quality. He turned to the first Cyberman. 'Is the force field operational?'

'The force field is in place, Cyberleader.'

'And the monitor?'

The Cyberman by the screen spoke in the same flat voice. 'The monitor is functional. If he comes, it will detect his alien form.'

'Report on the teleportation device?'

'It is functional, but its reliability is impaired.'

'It must be made reliable. The device is vital to us. If we are to gather equipment for the final plan...'

The first Cyberman spoke. 'We do not have the scientific knowledge to carry out the final plan. Without that knowledge, the equipment is useless.'

The second Cyberman said, 'The raids must be attracting human attention. Their forces will be seeking us.'

The first Cyberman carried on the gloomy chorus. 'The humans will notice the power losses from this base. We cannot conceal them forever. In time, they will use them to track us down. We are too few. We cannot defeat them.'

In a calm, passionless voice the Cyberleader said, 'All that you say is true. Our plan has only a small chance of success. But it is the only plan we have. We must carry it out to the end. We will survive.'

The first Cyberman said, 'Only the one who closed the Void has the knowledge to reopen it.'

The second Cyberman said, 'The one who

closed the Void is not here. He escaped from us.'

'He will return,' said the Cyberleader. 'We are attacking this planet. He has an emotional attachment to this planet. That is his weakness. He will hear of the attacks and return.'

Suddenly, a series of high-pitched beeps came from the monitor. A tiny point of light was pulsing on the screen.

'He has returned,' said the first Cyberman.

'Find precise location.'

'That will be difficult.'

'It must be done. For our plan to work, we need the Doctor.'

Hands in pockets, the Doctor wandered through the busy network of streets around the hospital. The rain had cleared up, the wind had dropped, and it was a pleasant sunny morning. And, somewhere, something mysterious was going on. That was what he liked about Earth. It was as unpredictable as its weather.

There was something very odd about those teleportation signals...

He found himself in a busy little street, lined with bookshops and cafés. One of the cafés bore a sign:

NICK'S INTERNET CAFE

'Aha!' said the Doctor out loud. 'Perfect!'

It was a small, fairly scruffy place. A glass-topped counter with a coffee machine behind it. Beyond, a double row of computers, a handful of them in use.

Behind the counter stood Nick himself, a small, thin, sad-looking man with a straggly goatee beard. He looked at the Doctor and said mournfully, 'Time?'

The Doctor nodded. 'Yes, well, that's the big question, isn't it? Time! You know what I always say? Time will tell. You have no idea how often that turns out to be the case.' He beamed at the café owner.

Nick sighed. 'How long?'

'Yeah, well, that's another one, isn't it.' He sucked air through his teeth. 'How long indeed? Who knows? From here to eternity. You know, Newton would say...' He frowned. 'I'm sorry – what was the question again?'

Nick was used to eccentrics. 'How long on the computer?' he asked patiently.

'Oh, about an hour should do.'

'Two quid. Cappuccino?'

'Definitely.'

'Another two quid.'

The Doctor searched through his pockets and eventually gathered together enough loose change to pay for his cappuccino and his computer time.

Nick pointed. 'That one there, end of the row.'

The Doctor carried his coffee over to the computer and sat down. For a moment or two, he sat staring vaguely at the keyboard.

At the next computer, a dark-haired girl, a law student researching her thesis, leant over and said, 'Need any help?'

The Doctor grinned. 'Thanks. But I think I can probably cope.' He pulled out his glasses and popped them on.

His long fingers flashed over the keyboard with amazing speed. A news channel appeared. The Doctor scrolled through it, speed-reading. He punched up another, then another and another. The girl raised her eyebrows and turned back to her own screen.

The Doctor sat back, thinking over what he had learned. The usual stuff. Worldwide wars, political struggles, show-business, celebrity gossip – humans didn't change much. And crime. In particular, robberies. Two of them – a computer store and a government lab. There was also one very brief report about an attack on an army camp, but the reports were curiously vague.

Even so, he now knew that three very well-protected establishments had been targeted, and there were no explanations of how the attackers got in, or how they escaped. To enter and leave a heavily guarded place without trace suggested something else: teleportation.

The Doctor thought for a moment, remembering a website he'd seen on an earlier visit to Earth. A website that dealt with the odd and the unexplained. Things like the Doctor himself, in fact. A website that provided strange reasons for strange events. Conspiracies.

His fingers moved over the keyboard again.

Just as he'd expected, all three raids figured largely on that website. There was even a special article about them. The article contained one vital fact, missing from all the earlier news reports the Doctor had read.

Giant silver figures had been sighted at all three raids. Reports of the sightings had been suppressed by the authorities, using all the powers of the state: D-notices, the Official Secrets Act, court injunctions... Witnesses who wouldn't keep quiet had simply vanished – many of them, it was suggested, into secure mental hospitals. There was, said the writer, only one possible explanation. The Cybermen were back, and the authorities were holding back the news to avoid panic.

The tone of the article was wild and hysterical, thought the Doctor, and the author might well be a little crazy. But he was right, all the same. The Cybermen were back. And if he knew about them, perhaps they knew about him. And Martha would soon be waiting by the TARDIS.

The Doctor jumped up and the pretty girl at the next screen looked round.

'Found all you wanted?'

'Oh yes. Rather more than I wanted, actually.' The Doctor gave her another smile, a rather sad one this time, and hurried out.

The girl watched him leave. 'Pity,' she thought. 'Completely bonkers, of course. But he looked rather interesting for a geek.'

She went back to her thesis.

CHAPTER SIX

REUNION

MARTHA JONES STOOD IN a familiar ward, soaking up the atmosphere. Nurses' station, nurses, medicine bottles and bedpans, bedside tables with flowers and fruit, a bed with the curtains drawn. Patients in various states of good and bad health, cheerfulness and misery. Strange how the really ill ones were often the most cheerful and uncomplaining. It was always the patients with in-growing toenails who gave the most trouble.

She was chatting to Rachel, a fellow medical student. Rachel was an old friend and had seemed pleased to see her, greeting her with a hug and squeals of delight. She seemed to have got over the ordeal of recent events at the hospital, almost to have forgotten it. Or rather, it was as if she didn't want to remember it, not in any detail.

Martha remembered what the Doctor had said in the car park.

'Oh yes, things are pretty well back to normal now,' said Rachel cheerfully. 'Same old grind. What about you? We were afraid you were dead, or had a breakdown or something.'

Martha realised she hadn't actually worked out a cover story. She laughed nervously. 'No, I'm fine.'

'Where did you get to? Where've you been all this time?'

Martha had to think fast. 'Well, I was pretty shaken up. I mean, we all were, weren't we? I just had to get away for a while...'

('And boy, did I get away!' she thought to herself.)

Rachel giggled. 'There were all sorts of rumours flying about. Some people said you'd gone off with the mystery man.'

'What mystery man?'

'Skinny bloke in a suit. The police were looking for him afterwards.'

Martha didn't know what to say.

'Anyway, when are you coming back?' Rachel went on.

'I'm not quite sure. Things aren't really sorted out yet.'

'Exams soon, remember. Have you been keeping up with the work?'

Martha laughed. 'Not exactly.'

She'd learned quite a lot while she'd been away, she thought. But most of it wasn't on any exam syllabus.

A commanding voice called from the end of the ward. 'Miss Swales? If you could spare me a moment?'

Rachel pulled a face. 'Chambers, he's starting his rounds. I must fly.'

'Me too,' said Martha. 'Look, don't tell anyone you've seen me, OK?'

As Rachel sped away, Martha hurried from the ward. It had been a mistake just dropping in like this, she thought. Bound to provoke lots of awkward questions.

She didn't want to get trapped in a lift with someone who knew her and would ask even more questions, so she took the stairs down to the busy main foyer and then headed for the car park.

To her relief the TARDIS was still standing in its place. At least the Doctor hadn't taken off, leaving her stranded on Earth.

'What do I mean, stranded?' she thought. Earth was her home. This hospital, this car park, were places where she belonged. The idea was strangely hard to accept. Was she becoming... There wasn't a word for it. A citizen of the cosmos? Like the Doctor... How long could she go on jaunting about through time and space with the Doctor? And how could she bear to stop?

It all needed a lot of thinking about. Leaning against the TARDIS, she settled down to wait.

Suddenly, the air in front of her seemed to shimmer. Martha rubbed her eyes and blinked, but the shimmering went on. Inside it, a shape began to form.

It was human-like – head, body, arms, legs – but far bigger than any human. It appeared to be made of metal, of gleaming steel. The massive body had a kind of chest unit with what looked like layered armour beneath. The head had tubes coming out of it like handles. The eyes were round holes, the mouth a narrow oblong slit.

Martha knew what it was. She had seen the terrifying shape on television and in countless newspaper photographs at the time of the invasion.

It was a Cyberman.

'Impossible, Doctor?' she thought. 'But here it is, large as life and twice as nasty! You've got some explaining to do.'

The Cyberman spoke. Its voice was metallic, flat, inhuman. 'Where is the Doctor?'

Martha gulped and swallowed. 'Who?'

'We have monitored a double heartbeat at this location. The Doctor has a double heartbeat. Where is the Doctor?'

'I don't know.'

'This box was seen inside the Torchwood Tower. Is the Doctor inside?'

'No, he's gone away.'

'Where has he gone?'

Martha was backing slowly away from the nightmare figure. 'Far away – for a long time,' she stammered, wishing it was true. But the Doctor might return at any moment – and he would be walking into an ambush.

The Cyberman stretched out an arm, and the barrel of a weapon clicked into place at the wrist.

'We need the Doctor. Without the Doctor you are useless to us. This is your final warning. Tell us where to find the Doctor or you will be deleted.'

CHAPTER SEVEN

CAUGHT

MARTHA STARED INTO THE dark barrel of the Cyberweapon.

If she spun round and ran, weaving from side to side... In her heart, she knew it would be useless. The Cyberman would simply shoot her down. Still, it was better than standing still to be shot. She tensed, ready to leap aside – and an indignant voice shouted, 'Oi, you!'

The Doctor stepped out from behind a van.

The Cyberman whirled round, with its arm still raised. The Cyberweapon was aimed directly at the Doctor.

'Look out, Doctor!' shouted Martha.

'Just stay where you are,' the Doctor told her calmly, before ducking back out of sight behind the van. The Cyberman strode after him.

There followed a deadly game of hide-and-seek between the rows of parked cars. The Doctor's aim was simple – to dodge around the Cyberman and reach the TARDIS.

The Cyberman, however, was clearly well aware of this. Whenever the Doctor made a dash for the police box, the Cyberman was there ahead of him.

But the Doctor was quicker and more agile than the Cyberman, and finally he got his chance. He faked a move to the left, moved to the right, dodged around the Cyberman and sprinted towards Martha and the box, reaching for the TARDIS key as he ran.

Martha looked on anxiously, poised to leap into the TARDIS the moment the Doctor opened the door.

Then, to her horror, the air between them started to shimmer...

Suddenly a second Cyberman appeared, and the Doctor ran straight into its arms. It held him in an immensely powerful grip. The Doctor struggled furiously, but it was no use.

The first Cyberman marched towards them.

Martha froze in horror, unsure what to do.

'Run, Martha!' shouted the Doctor.

The air shimmered again and, to the Doctor's astonishment, the fierce grip on his arms was gone. The Cyberman holding him had simply disappeared. So had the other one.

Shaking his head in amazement, the Doctor hurried over to Martha, who stood looking at him as if stunned.

'You all right?' he asked.

'Oh yes,' she said calmly. 'Attacked by alien monsters – happens every day. Actually,' she decided, 'I think it does happen every day. You OK?'

'Oh, I'm fine. Let's get away from here.'

'What a good idea!'

Martha moved towards the TARDIS door, but the Doctor shook his head.

'Not yet. One or two things round here need looking into. Actually, not just round here. Actually, not just one or two either. Tell you what...'

'What?'

'I could do with a nice cup of tea.'

'Typical,' thought Martha. 'Just when you want to go, he wants to stay.'

Out loud, she said, 'I know just the place.'

They found a corner table in the busy hospital canteen and sat down with their teas.

'Now then,' said Martha. 'Explanation time. Where did those Cybermen come from? And why did they disappear?'

'I can make a guess at the second question. Their transportation system is on the blink. I don't remember the Cybermen being able to teleport, so it may be alien technology – alien to Cybermen, I mean. Probably overdue a service. And I'm guessing they don't have a maintenance agreement with Teleports R Us, first and best in teleport repair and conditioning. As for where they came from...'

'You said it was impossible for there to be any more Cybermen on Earth,' said Martha accusingly.

'It is.'

'But there they were.'

'There they were,' agreed the Doctor.

'So you were wrong.'

'I'm never wrong,' said the Doctor simply. 'I'm a genius.'

'But—'

The Doctor held up his hand. 'What I actually said, or at least, what I actually *meant*, or at least what I actually meant to say, was that it's impossible for any of the Cybermen who invaded from the Void to be still on Earth.'

'Why?'

'They were all contaminated with Void material, and I fixed it so they'd all be sucked back into the Void.' He shot his arm out to demonstrate. 'Shumm. Like that.'

'So those two were the first of a new lot – scouts for an invading army.'

The Doctor shook his head. 'No,' he said definitely. 'It's impossible for any more Cybermen to break through. I told you, the gap into the Void is sealed forever.' Once again that expression of sadness passed over the Doctor's face.

'But, that's a good thing, isn't it?' asked Martha. 'The gap being permanently sealed.'

'I suppose so.'

'Then why are you looking so glum about it?'

'Personal reasons,' said the Doctor briefly. He brought his attention back to the present.

'Anyway,' Martha was saying, 'according to you, none of the old lot of invading Cybermen can still be here.'

'That's right.'

'And no new ones can have arrived?'

'Impossible.'

'Then how can those two we saw be here? I mean, unless they were here all along—'

She broke off. The Doctor was staring at her, wide-eyed.

'That's it! Home-made! Hey, perhaps you're a genius too.'

'Thanks. Doctor—'

'Even before they finally invaded, the Cybermen had established a base inside the

Torchwood Tower at Canary Wharf. They were making new Cybermen there. They must have made some using purely Earth materials. Stuff they found here. This lot have never passed through the Void.' The Doctor thought of the accounts of the raids he'd found on the Internet. 'There can only be a few of them...'

'Just as well.' Martha paused. 'You were there, weren't you, at the final battle?'

The Doctor nodded.

'My cousin – Adeola. She worked at Torchwood Tower. She never came home after...' Martha sighed. 'I just wondered if you might have seen her. She looked a bit like me.'

The Doctor didn't answer. He was staring across the canteen. But what he saw in his mind's eye was a dark-skinned girl sitting rigidly upright at a control console. He saw her earpiece being wrenched away, the fleshy Cyber-filament being tugged out from deep inside her brain. He'd freed her and several of her colleagues from Cyber-control – and killed them in the process.

Martha was watching the expression on the Doctor's face.

'What is it, Doctor?'

With an effort, the Doctor pushed the terrible memory aside. 'Things were pretty chaotic there at the end. A lot of people died. I'm sorry, Martha.'

Martha would have asked more questions, but suddenly she heard a voice calling her from across the room. 'Martha – over here!'

Martha jumped up. 'It's Rachel, an old mate of mine. We were talking earlier. I'll get rid of her, but I'll have to chat to her for a few minutes.'

The Doctor nodded as if he had barely heard her, and Martha hurried away. He sat staring into his plastic cup of cold tea. He needed to find out more about what was going on...

Then a shadow fell over him. He looked up and saw an attractive fair-haired girl in army uniform. She was flanked by two very large, red-capped military policeman, both armed with revolvers.

'I am Captain Sheila Sarandon,' she said crisply. 'And you are the Doctor.' It was a statement, not a question.

The Doctor looked thoughtfully at her. This didn't look too good.

'There are lots of doctors here,' he said mildly. 'It is a hospital after all.'

She gave him a wintry smile. 'Ah, but you're *the* Doctor. The one we want. You're under arrest.'

CHAPTER EIGHT

ARREST

THE DOCTOR LEANED BACK in his rickety plastic chair, glancing idly around the canteen. His eyes passed over Martha, who had stopped talking to the girl in the tea queue and was looking at him in alarm. She started to move towards him and he gave a tiny shake of his head.

On the other side of the room Martha picked up the signal. No use both of them getting scooped up by the authorities. She turned to Rachel. 'Lend me your coat, quick. Just for a moment.'

Puzzled, Rachel took off the white coat, and Martha slipped into it. She saw a familiar figure just ahead of her in the queue and tapped him on the shoulder.

'Fanshawe! How's it going?'

The young man, another fellow medical student, turned and looked at her in amazement. 'Martha, what are you doing here? Are you back with us?'

'Not exactly. That a new stethoscope?' she asked. 'Let's have a look!'

She slipped it from around his neck, put it on and pretended to listen to his heart.

Rachel had been watching all this. 'What's going on Martha? Is that your mysterious friend over there with those army types? He seems to be in trouble.'

'He usually is,' said Martha. 'Look, I can't explain right now. Just keep chatting, OK, so I can blend in with the crowd.'

At his table, the Doctor was still playing for time.

'So what am I charged with? I do have rights, you know.'

'I doubt it, Doctor,' said the young woman 'You're not a citizen, are you? According to the confidential files, you're not even human. Let's just say it's a matter of national security.'

'Planetary security might be more accurate.' The Doctor stood up. 'All right, if we're going, let's go.'

'And no trouble,' said one of the two massive military policemen.

The Doctor looked thoughtfully at him. As it happened, the Doctor was quite keen to get in contact with the authorities – on his own terms.

This seemed as good a way as any.

Captain Sarandon said, 'By the way, where's your companion?'

The Doctor looked puzzled. 'Companion?'

'According to the files, there's always a companion. Usually an attractive young female. Where is she?'

'I've no idea what you're talking about,' said the Doctor. 'But you can be my companion if you like.' He watched her expression change to a frown. 'OK, so you don't like. The job's still vacant then.'

Captain Sarandon looked around the busy canteen. It was crowded with doctors, nurses, medical students and patients. There were quite a few attractive young females among them.

'Never mind, we'll pick her up later. Come along, Doctor.'

She led the way out of the canteen, and the Doctor followed, flanked by the two military policemen. They crossed the foyer and left the hospital. As they reached the top of the hospital steps, the Doctor couldn't help glancing towards the car park.

'Don't worry about your TARDIS, Doctor,' said Captain Sarandon. 'It's being taken care of. It'll reach Chadwick Green soon after us.'

She led him across the car park to the spot

where he had left the TARDIS. A lorry with built-in lifting gear, the kind used to take away illegally parked cars, stood next to the police box. Men in denim overalls were fitting padded clamps around it.

'Should have bought that ticket after all,' said the Doctor. He grinned at the men. 'Handle her with care, won't you. She's not as young as she used to be. But then, who is?'

'This way, Doctor,' said Captain Sarandon. She led him to an army staff car parked nearby. One of the military policemen climbed into the back seat, and the second signalled to the Doctor to follow him. He got in, and the second policeman followed. The Doctor was sandwiched between them.

Captain Sarandon took the seat beside the driver, and the staff car swept away.

'So, where and what is Chadwick Green?' asked the Doctor, as they drove out of the car park.

'Army research centre, just outside London,' said Captain Sarandon. 'No more questions till we arrive, please, Doctor – then we'll be asking them.'

'Oh, now that's a surprise. Big surprise that is. Surprise so big you could paint it red and call it a bus – oof!'

The policeman on his left had given him a painful elbow jab in the ribs.

'You heard the officer – shut it!'

The Doctor shut it, and the staff car sped on its way.

In the vast, shadowy chamber where the Cybermen had set up their base, the three Cybermen were debating in their cold, unfeeling way.

'You have failed in your duty,' the Cyberleader told the Cyber-engineer. 'The teleport failed at a vital moment. Transmission focus was lost. The Doctor was in our hands. Now he has escaped us.'

'The scanning equipment has also failed,' said the second Cyberman. 'We cannot locate the Doctor.'

The Cyber-engineer said emotionlessly, 'I informed you that this alien machine was unreliable. You did not take that fact into account in your plans. You have failed in your duty as leader.'

'Do not dispute my authority or you will be deleted.'

'We are only three,' the Cyber-engineer reminded him. 'To reduce our number to two would be inefficient.'

'Then we must adapt our plan,' the other Cyberman said.

There was a moment of silence as the Cyberleader processed these words. Then he said, 'Have you repaired the teleportation equipment?'

'Limited function will soon be restored.'

'We will test it with another transmission.'

'Transmitting only one of us will reduce the strain on the focus equipment.'

'When the teleport is repaired you will transmit me back to the same place,' ordered the Cyberleader. 'The Doctor may still be in the area. His capture is essential.'

CHAPTER NINE

INTERROGATION

THE DOCTOR WAS BEING driven through the gates of Chadwick Green Research Centre. The car drove along the edge of the parade ground and drew up close to one of the larger huts.

'Out!' ordered one of the military policemen. He got out of the car, and the second policeman shoved the Doctor out after him.

Captain Sarandon stood waiting. She slapped the roof of the car and it drove away. 'Come along, Doctor. Major Burton's waiting.'

'Just a moment, Captain,' said the Doctor. There was an unexpected note of authority in his voice.

'What is it?' she said impatiently.

The Doctor nodded towards the military policeman who had jabbed him in the car. 'One of your men is a bit too free with his hands – or rather, his elbow. My ribs are still sore.'

Captain Sarandon looked at the man. 'Well?'

'No idea what he's talking about ma'am. We

were a bit crowded in the back, I might have jostled him accidentally.'

'You see, Doctor? Just an accident.'

'It was nothing of the kind,' said the Doctor angrily. 'It was a deliberate assault. An assault on my ribs.'

Sheila Sarandon sighed. 'If you'd care to make an official complaint, I'll see it's investigated.'

'Once I've filled in a dozen forms, I bet. Still, I don't think we need be too formal about a little matter like this,' said the Doctor. 'I'd sooner deal with it informally.'

'And how do you propose to do that?'

'Like this,' said the Doctor.

He reached up – he had to reach up since the man towered above him – and pulled the offending policeman's nose. He didn't pull it very hard. But there was something scornful about the gesture that made it completely infuriating.

With a roar of rage, the policeman hurled himself at the Doctor.

Sheila Sarandon wasn't quite clear about what happened next, even though it took place right in front of her. Somehow, the man missed his target and ended up in a heap on the ground, his revolver now in the Doctor's hand and covering the little group.

The policeman stopped and looked to his officer for orders.

Captain Sarandon did her best to hide her shock. 'You can't hope to escape, Doctor.'

'Oh, I don't want to escape,' said the Doctor. 'I'm just protecting my ribs. Well, maybe I'm making a bit of a point as well.' He gestured with the revolver. 'Get him on his feet. He's not badly hurt.'

The policeman helped his colleague to rise.

'Right,' said the Doctor. He paused, seeming to notice the gun in his hand for the first time. 'Yes,' he decided, 'I think you'd better look after this.' And he handed it to Sarandon. 'Now, let's go and see this Major What's-his-name.'

Sarandon stared at the gun she was now holding in surprise. 'Major Burton,' she answered automatically.

The Doctor grinned. 'Right – let's go for a Burton.'

Major Burton looked up as Captain Sarandon came into his office, followed by two military policemen. Behind them came a thin, youngish man with untidy dark hair wearing a rather scruffy pinstriped suit.

Major Burton gave no sign of surprise. He rose politely from behind his desk.

'Ah, Captain Sarandon. You've brought a visitor to see me.'

'It might be more accurate to say that he brought us, sir,' said Sheila Sarandon ruefully.

The Doctor grinned affably. 'Just helping out.' He turned to the military policemen. 'Now, then, you two – why don't you clear off and study the Geneva Convention or something. The bit about the treatment of prisoners is instructive.'

The two policemen looked at Major Burton, who nodded briefly. They saluted and marched out.

'Now then,' said the Doctor briskly, 'I take it you're Major Burton. You're in charge here?'

'I like to think so.'

'And I like to think that I'm the Doctor.'

'I rather gathered that.'

'You want to talk to me and I want to talk to you, so let's not waste any more time. Oh, and how about some tea and sandwiches before we start? I seem to have missed lunch.'

It took some time for Martha to get away from Rachel and Fanshawe. They were full of questions, none of which she really wanted to answer. Where had she been? Who was her friend? And why had he been arrested? But she

53

broke away at last, promising to return later and explain everything.

It was only as she was hurrying down the hospital steps that she realised that she had no idea where to go, or what to do next. She could go to the police, tell them what had happened and demand to be put in touch with the Doctor. Or she could go back to her family – and face still more uncomfortable questions. Still she had to sleep somewhere that night, and at least they'd give her a meal...

She decided to wait by the TARDIS. If the Doctor escaped or talked his way out of trouble, he'd be certain to go back there. But, when she reached the spot, the TARDIS was gone.

Martha stared at the blank space in shock. Had the Doctor gone off in it? Not with his military escort, surely. More likely the Army had taken it. Since they'd scooped up the Doctor, they might well have grabbed the TARDIS too. So now what was she to do? She'd just about decided on family as the least bad of her choices when the decision was taken for her.

The air before her shimmered... Seeing the danger, she turned to run, but it was already too late. A Cyberman appeared before her and clasped her in a steely embrace.

Martha struggled for a moment, but it was no

use. 'Shall we dance?' she said.

A tall, blue-clad figure stepped out from between the cars – PC Jim Wilkie, making yet another of his routine patrols. He saw a girl struggling in the grip of a giant silver figure and yelled, 'Hey! Stop that! Let her go!'

But it was too late. The girl and her attacker simply faded away.

PC Wilkie groaned and mopped his brow. What was the desk sergeant going to make of this?

CHAPTER TEN

THE DOCTOR TAKES CHARGE

THE DOCTOR WAS SITTING, very much at his ease, in the visitor's chair in front of Major Burton's desk, finishing the last of a plate of ham sandwiches.

Major Burton watched him thoughtfully. He was a patient man when he needed to be. If the Doctor was prepared to be cooperative, he was willing to treat him as a guest, not a prisoner.

The Doctor swallowed the last bite of his sandwich and washed it down with a swig from his mug of tea.

'My compliments to the cook-house,' he said indistinctly. 'Now, let's get to the real meat, shall we? Why have I been brought here?'

'To answer questions, not ask them,' snapped Sheila Sarandon.

Major Burton held up his hand to silence her. 'There have been a number of curious and unexplained incidents recently, Doctor,' he said. 'I'm not sure if I'm allowed to tell you about them.'

'Then why bring me here? Bit of a waste of time all round, if you ask me.' The Doctor stood up. 'But that's your problem. I'll be off then, shall I?' He waited a moment, enjoying their confused reactions, then sat down again. 'Don't worry. I already know. You're concerned about a series of raids on technology and research centres – including this base. Am I right or am I right?'

'How the devil—'

The Doctor ignored the interruption. 'All the raids were on well-protected, well-guarded places, which were entered with no alarms triggered and no traces of a break-in. In each raid, advanced electronic equipment was stolen.'

'You're very well informed,' said Major Burton.

'Suspiciously well informed,' said Captain Sarandon. 'Where did you learn all this?'

The Doctor waved at the computer on the desk. 'On the Internet, like everybody else. I learned something else as well. It seems very likely that the raids were carried out by Cybermen.'

'That information is classified,' said Sheila Sarandon angrily.

'Is it? Well, it's also on every conspiracy site on the Web. You still haven't answered *my* question.'

'What question?'

'Why did you bring me here?'

It was Major Burton who answered him. 'After the recent alien invasions, the authorities issued a series of confidential reports. The reports leave out a lot of information but, reading between the lines, it seems clear that someone called the Doctor had a lot to do with defeating the invasion.'

'I suppose that's true,' said the Doctor modestly. 'Well, it was all me, really. Most of the time, everyone else just got in the way. People do that. So, are you arresting me or what?'

'In my view, this is a Military Intelligence matter,' said Major Burton stiffly. 'I should prefer to deal with it myself.'

The Doctor laughed. 'Makes sense. Rivalry between different agencies. You want something to boast about at the Intelligence Organisations' Christmas Party.'

Sheila Sarandon interrupted him. 'Let's stick to the Cybermen, shall we Doctor? Since you seem to know so much about them.'

'Just a bit. Big bit, actually. Well, rather a lot really,' said the Doctor. 'I take it you brought me here to ask for my help.'

'Well, yes...'

'And, in order to persuade me to give you that help, you had me arrested in public, thrown in a car with a couple of gorillas and whizzed down here. Oh, and elbowed in the ribs. Don't forget I was elbowed in the ribs.'

'I'm sorry if you feel our methods were abrupt, Doctor,' said Major Burton. 'But there is a crisis.'

The Doctor thought for a moment. It seemed to Sheila Sarandon that, somehow, he had taken charge. *They* were waiting on *his* decision...

'Yeah, all right,' said the Doctor. 'I'll help you. But on certain conditions. I want a completely free hand, no more of this under-arrest nonsense. Nothing more in the ribs either. I won't have that.'

'Very well,' said Major Burton.

'Sir, is that wise?' protested Captain Sarandon.

'That's my decision, Captain,' said Major Burton. 'I'm impressed with the Doctor's grasp of what has happened. If he plays ball with me, I'll play ball with him.'

'Oh, I used to like a game of cricket,' said the Doctor. 'Mind you, I'd like you to do something for me.' He turned to Sheila Sarandon. 'You were quite right, I do have a companion. Or "friend", as you Earth People say when you're speaking proper English. Her name's Martha Jones.' He gave a brief description of Martha. 'She made herself scarce when you picked me up. I'd like you to find her and bring her down here. Approach her nicely. Tell her she can ring me here if she's worried.'

'I'll get on to it,' said Sheila Sarandon. 'It'll be quickest if I send a staff car.'

She moved over to her desk and picked up the phone.

'Tell them to mind her ribs,' the Doctor said.

When she'd finished the call, Sarandon turned back to the Doctor. 'Now then, Doctor, as Major Burton said, there is a crisis.'

'Well, sort of. There is and there isn't,' said the Doctor.

'And what's that supposed to mean?'

'There is a crisis, yes – but it may not be as bad as you think.'

Major Burton sighed. 'Looks pretty bad to me. Perhaps you'd explain that.'

The Doctor got up and began pacing up and down the office. 'You're afraid that these raids are the start of another full-scale Cyberman invasion?'

'Well, aren't they?'

'No,' said the Doctor firmly. 'Another invasion is impossible.'

'Why?' asked Sheila Sarandon doubtfully.

'The Cybermen invaded Earth from another dimension – they came through something called the Void. I defeated their invasion by having them all sucked back into the Void and sealing the gateway between that dimension and ours forever. They can never return to Earth.'

'But they have! They're here.'

'They didn't invade. They were here all along,' said the Doctor. 'A handful of Cybermen were created here on Earth. They weren't sucked into the Void with the others, because they were never contaminated by it.'

Major Burton said, 'A stay-behind group. With a hidden base, supplies, weapons... We planned to do the same thing in 1940 if the Nazis invaded. And the Nazis *did* do it, in 1945, when we invaded Germany. Called themselves Werewolves.'

The Doctor stopped pacing and perched on the corner of Major Burton's desk.

'Whatever we call them, we still have a problem,' he said. 'Even a small group of Cybermen can do an awful lot of damage.'

'What makes you so sure it's a small group?' demanded Sheila. 'Even if your theory's right, they could have an army hidden away.'

'They didn't have the time, or the resources,' said the Doctor. Without anyone noticing, he had taken over the meeting. 'Or any reason to, come to that. They didn't know they were going to be sucked into the Void – not until it was too late. Bit of a daft plan if they did. No, I'm pretty sure there are no more than a handful of them.'

'Why?' asked Sheila again.

'Cybermen always attack in large numbers – if they can,' said the Doctor. 'Yet nobody's ever seen more than two of this lot at the same time. Say there's at least one left at their base to operate the transmission equipment – there could be no more than three of them. Maybe one or two in reserve.'

Major Burton was looking a lot more cheerful. 'Let's hope you're right, Doctor. I think we can deal with a mere handful of Cybermen, however powerful they are. So, all we need to know now is – where are they?'

'And what do they want?' added Sheila.

'Oh, we know that,' said the Doctor. 'We know what they want. What they want's obvious – they want me.'

He told them of the attempt to kidnap him.

'Why should they want you?' asked Sheila.

'Oh thanks. Big ego-boost that was. But

actually, for the same reason as you do. They think I can help them.'

'How?'

'As you said yourself, it's a question of what they want,' said the Doctor. 'Knowing the Cybermen, their only aim is conquest. They know they can't conquer the Earth with only a few of them. I rather imagine they want me to open up the gateway to the Void again and bring back their Cyber-army.'

CHAPTER ELEVEN

HOSTAGE

THE BRIEF BLUR OF teleportation faded, and Martha Jones stood looking around her in amazement. She was in a vast shadowy hall of some kind. A domed roof, supported by struts and cables, was just visible high overhead. Electronic equipment had been assembled in a small, lighted area. It was tended by two giant steel figures.

The Cyberman that had brought her released its grip and thrust Martha towards the others. 'This female is known to the Doctor.'

'You were instructed to bring the Doctor.'

'The Doctor was not to be found. Transmission time was limited. The human female was there, so I brought her.'

'We have no use for her.'

Martha found that anger was rapidly replacing fear. 'I've not much use for you lot either,' she said angrily.

Ignoring her, the Cybermen went on discussing her in their flat, metallic voices.

'It is possible that she knows where the Doctor may be found.'

'Ask her.'

The Cyberman who'd captured her swung round, looming over her. 'Where is the Doctor?'

'No idea.'

'Tell us, or you will be deleted.'

'Killed, you mean?'

'That is correct.'

'If you kill me, I won't be able to tell you anything.'

'Tell us where to find the Doctor,' ordered the Cyberman.

'I don't know where he is.'

A massive metal hand took her elbow in a claw-like grip. 'Tell us where the Doctor is, or I will cause you pain.'

The grip clamped harder. Martha bit her lip, determined not to scream. 'Humans are fragile,' she said with an effort. 'If you hurt me, I will die.'

'Since you will not speak, we lose nothing by killing you,' said the Cyberman. It turned to the one who seemed to be the leader. 'Shall I delete her?'

The Cyberleader considered – for what seemed to Martha a very long time. 'No,' he said at last.

'When we find the Doctor, she will be a useful hostage.'

The Cyberman holding Martha released its grip and turned away.

Martha stood rubbing her sore elbow, looking around her. She was overcome by a strange feeling. She was pretty sure she had been here before. But not with the place like this – a dark, empty shell. When she'd been here before, there had been lights and music, clowns and aerial dancers, exhibitions and installations and cafés and food stalls. There had been a whole fairground.

She'd come as a stroppy teenager, dragged there by her mum and dad, still together then. She'd quite enjoyed it, although she'd refused to admit it.

'I'm in the Dome,' she realised. 'The Cybermen's secret base is the Millennium Dome!'

The Doctor, Major Burton and Captain Sarandon stood watching as a duty corporal finished pinning a scale map of Greater London to the map board on the office wall.

'Thank you, Corporal,' said Major Burton.

'Sir,' barked the soldier. He saluted and marched out.

'It's hopeless,' said Sheila Sarandon. 'They could be anywhere on this map.'

'Or off it,' said Major Burton. 'We've no guarantee they're in this area at all. They could be anywhere between Land's End and John O'Groats.'

The Doctor shook his head. 'I doubt it.'

Sheila Sarandon asked her usual question. 'Why?'

'For one thing, their teleportation equipment isn't very reliable. It failed when they tried to capture us. I don't think they'd trust it any further than they could throw a rat. Mind you, Cybermen – good throwing arms. Still quite a way. But they broke out from Torchwood Tower, remember. I think we're looking for the first good hiding place close to Canary Wharf.'

'And how do we find it?'

'Power,' said the Doctor. 'They'd need massive amounts, and they must be stealing it.' He paused for a moment to think. 'Unless they have thousands of highly trained hamsters going round in special wheels... No,' he decided. 'Definitely stealing it. So, if we can trace the electricity leakage...'

'I'll get on to the Grid,' said Sheila Sarandon. She went over to her phone. But it rang before she could pick it up.

'Hello... Yes... Yes, I see. Thank you.' Sheila turned to the Doctor and Burton. 'My people have checked all over the Royal Hope and couldn't find your friend, although several people remembered talking to her. But...' She hesitated.

The Doctor saw the look on her face. 'But what?'

'A policeman reported a strange event in the car park. A silver giant grabbing a girl – then they both vanished.'

'She went back to the TARDIS and found it had gone,' said the Doctor. 'While she was there a Cyberman turned up, looking for me – and settled for Martha.' He began pacing up and down again, thinking aloud. 'She can't tell them anything. She doesn't know where I am. They might just kill her, but there's a chance they'll keep her as a hostage... Ah!' He stopped pacing, and pointed at the desk. 'Can I use your phone?' He beamed at Major Burton and Captain Sarandon. 'I keep forgetting how technologically advanced you humans are these days!'

'Do you think she'll be able to answer?' asked Sheila Sarandon as she watched the Doctor dialling Martha's mobile number.

'If she's still alive,' said the Doctor quietly.

CHAPTER TWELVE

ATTACK

IN THE ECHOING GLOOM of the Dome, Martha studied the group of Cybermen. They were clustered around their equipment and seemed to be ignoring her for the moment.

Maybe this was her chance. Martha was determined to do *something*. She certainly wasn't going to mope around, waiting for someone to come and rescue her.

She started to edge slowly away. From what she remembered, the Dome was huge. Maybe she could get away, hide somewhere. Perhaps she could even escape. If she could find the Doctor and tell him of the Cybermen's base... She moved a little further away.

A metallic voice boomed, 'Do not move or you will be deleted.'

Martha shrugged and stood still, waiting for another chance.

When her mobile phone rang, it seemed so normal that she answered automatically.

'Hello?'

The Doctor's voice rang out clearly. 'Martha – how lovely to hear your voice. I'm at Chadwick Green Research Centre. So, where the devil are you?'

'I'm in the Do—'

A giant metal hand reached out and snatched the phone, crushing it into metal fragments.

'Excellent,' said the Cyberleader. 'That is all we need to know. Prepare the attack squad for revival.'

The Doctor looked at his dead phone for a moment and put it away.

'What did she say?' asked Sheila Sarandon.

'Just one syllable,' said the Doctor. '"Doh". As in "doh, re, mi".' He went back to the map and studied it thoughtfully.

'I spy with my little eye... something beginning with doh...' His pointing finger shot out. 'And there it is! "Doh", as in "Doh, how could I have been so stupid?" The Dome! The good old Millennium Dome! Big, deserted, lots of power outlets – and conveniently close to Canary Wharf. Well, at least someone's found a use for it at last.'

Martha stood watching as two of the Cybermen

dragged a coffin-shaped metal box up to the equipment complex and attached electrodes to the sides. The box hummed with power and a giant steel shape sat up inside like a corpse waking from the dead. Or like Frankenstein's monster coming to life in an old horror movie.

The Cyberman climbed stiffly from the container and stood upright. Its metal arm clanged across its armoured chest in salute. Then it moved aside and another container was dragged forward.

Martha watched, horrified and fascinated, as the process was repeated again and again, until four more Cybermen had been revived from hibernation.

The Cyberleader reviewed his troops.

'Soon we shall be ready for transmission. The Doctor must be captured alive. Other life forms may be deleted.'

Martha wondered if these were all the Cybermen that had been held in reserve. Five in all and, with the original three, eight – unless they had a whole army stashed away. Though, according to the Doctor, they wouldn't have had time...

She stepped forward. 'Are these all you have?'

'They will be sufficient.'

The Cyberleader turned to the original two Cybermen. 'One of you will operate the teleport mechanism. The other will guard the prisoner. We shall return with the Doctor.'

A circle of light appeared in the centre of the equipment complex. One by one, the Cybermen stepped into it and faded away. The Cyberleader waited till last.

'What good will it do you to capture the Doctor anyway?' said Martha as he prepared to depart. 'He won't help you.'

'The Doctor will obey our orders,' said the Cyberleader.

'Why should he?'

'If he does not help us, he will see you die.'

Major Burton was in his element, barking orders into the telephone and busily assembling an assault force to attack the Dome.

The Doctor looked on, his face grave. He seemed to be waiting for something.

'Don't spread your forces too thin, Major,' he warned. 'I'd keep some men here to guard this base.'

'They won't attack us here,' said the Major confidently. 'We have the upper hand now. We know where they are. They'll soon be on the defensive.'

'We may know where they are,' said Sheila Sarandon. 'But don't forget they know where you are, Doctor.'

'True,' he admitted.

'Because you told them,' said Sheila Sarandon.

'Oh yes. I did, didn't I?' said the Doctor.

'Why? You didn't have to.'

He sniffed. 'It just seemed like a good idea at the time.'

'But... If they know where you are, and if they desperately need your help, isn't it possible they'll try to come and get you?'

The Doctor made a point of seeming surprised. 'You really think so? Well, yes, I suppose it's possible. Maybe you'd better take precautions.'

The Major looked worried. 'It'll take some time for the attack force to assemble. If they attack us again here...' He smiled. 'Even if they do, we'll cope. I made some extra preparations after the last attack, applied for some special equipment.'

The sound of a shot came from outside the office, then another. Then a volley of shots and the blare of an alarm.

They rushed to the door, and looked out – to see a line of steel figures advancing across the parade ground.

CHAPTER THIRTEEN

BATTLEGROUND

THE DOCTOR SURVEYED THE advancing group. 'Six of them,' he said. 'And one or two more back at base.'

Shots rang out, as soldiers fired from the shelter of the nearby buildings. Bullets bounced off the armoured bodies of the attackers. The Cybermen ignored them and continued their steady advance. Red flares of energy pulsed from their wrist-guns. A soldier screamed, twisted and fell.

Major Burton and Captain Sarandon drew their revolvers and joined the defence. Their bullets, like those of the soldiers, had no effect.

'Rifles and revolvers won't do any good,' called the Doctor.

'So we've just discovered,' said Major Burton grimly. 'But don't worry, Doctor. I told you, I ordered some special equipment.' He raised his voice in a parade-ground bellow. 'Special squad forward.'

Two men rushed forward from between two of the buildings. They wore heavy packs and carried a sort of giant metal tube between them. In what was obviously a well-rehearsed action, one soldier knelt down, and the other helped him to shoulder the tube. Then the second man knelt behind the first and adjusted the giant tube, using his fellow as an aiming platform.

'Latest ground-to-ground rocket launcher,' said the Major. 'Reloadable, uses high-explosive shells. Still in the experimental stage. But they claim it'll take out a tank.'

When the tube was ready, the first soldier held it steady while the second pulled a firing handle set into the weapon's side.

A fiery streak shot across the parade ground, striking a Cyberman full in the chest. The results were immediate and spectacular. The Cyberman exploded in a ball of flame, and a shower of metal fragments rained down on the parade ground.

A ragged cheer went up from the surrounding soldiers.

'Reload,' bellowed Major Burton.

The second soldier took a shell from the pack and loaded it into the tube.

'Fire!' shouted Major Burton.

He was too late. Several energy blasts

converged on the weapon and it exploded, killing both soldiers.

'Second squad forward,' shouted Major Burton. 'Fire and take cover!'

Another two-man team appeared, aimed their weapon and fired. A second Cyberman was destroyed, and the team darted back into cover between the buildings.

With incredible speed they reloaded and fired again, blowing up another Cyberman.

'Three down, three to go,' said Major Burton. 'I told you we'd cope, Doctor.'

He had spoken too soon. As the second team darted from cover to fire for the third time, all three surviving Cybermen fired at once. Like the first, the second weapon exploded, killing its crew.

'How many more of those things have you got?' asked the Doctor.

'Just one. It'll have to be enough.' Major Burton raised his voice. 'Third squad forward!'

The arrival of the third squad seemed to take the Cybermen by surprise, and yet another Cyberman was blasted into nothingness. But the shot alerted the two survivors, and they both turned and fired, killing both soldiers. Somehow, the weapon escaped most of the impact and rolled across the parade ground.

The two remaining Cybermen advanced.

Suddenly Major Burton leaped from the shelter of the doorway, dashed across the parade ground, grabbed the weapon and the fallen shell-pack and carried them into cover. Even for a man his size, it was an incredible feat of strength.

'It takes two to fire it,' shouted Captain Sarandon. She started to follow him.

But the Doctor was ahead of her. Dodging between the pulses from the Cybermen's guns, he ran behind the building. Major Burton was loading the rocket launcher and struggling to raise it to his shoulder. The Doctor helped him, then knelt behind the Major, steadying the launcher.

'Firing lever – on the side,' gasped Burton.

The Doctor found it – just as a Cyberman came round the corner of the hut. For a moment, the Doctor paused. He looked at the Cyberman, thought about the human being it had once been – a thinking, feeling, *real* person. But no more. That person was dead already.

The Doctor and the Cyberman fired at the same instant. The Cyberman exploded, and so did the launcher. The Doctor, leaping aside as soon as he'd fired, was knocked off his feet by the blast.

Major Burton was not so lucky. His body lay slumped across the shattered remains of the weapon.

The Doctor struggled to his feet and staggered over to him. He knelt beside the body, felt for a pulse and found nothing.

The Doctor straightened up just as the Cyberleader, the only Cyberman to survive the battle, appeared around the corner of the hut.

The Cyberleader raised his arm, and the Doctor gazed into the barrel of the Cyberweapon attached to its wrist...

CHAPTER FOURTEEN

THE GATEWAY

FOR A LONG MOMENT the two confronted each other.

The Cyberleader scanned the Doctor intently. 'You are the Doctor.'

'You're not wrong, you know. I *am* the Doctor.'

'You must help us.'

'You could be wrong now, though. Must I?'

'Your female associate is our prisoner at the place humans call the Dome. Come to us there and help us, or she will die.' As he finished speaking, the air around the Cyberleader shimmered and he faded away.

Captain Sarandon came round the corner, revolver in hand, just as the Cyberleader disappeared.

'Well, that was the last of them.'

'For the moment,' said the Doctor. 'There are more of them at the Dome. I'm not sure how many.'

'The assault force will deal with them.' She looked down at Major Burton's body. 'Is he dead?'

'I'm afraid so.'

She nodded, accepting the loss as soldiers do. 'He was very brave. Posthumous VC, I shouldn't wonder. You were brave too, helping him.'

'Was I? Guns aren't brave, you know.'

'All the same, I'm grateful.'

'What will you do now?'

'Join up with the assault force and finish the job for him.'

The Doctor looked her in the eyes. 'If you attack the Dome in force, you'll lose more men.'

'It goes with the job.'

'I can't let you do it. My friend Martha is a prisoner there. The Cybermen will kill her as soon as the battle starts. They've no use for prisoners.'

'I'm sorry, Doctor, what else can I do? It's not just your friend who's in danger.'

'You can trust me,' said the Doctor.

'What do you mean?'

'You said you were grateful – then do something for me. You've got my TARDIS here?'

'Yes, it's in the security vault.'

'Take me to it. If you do, there's a chance I

can save Martha and dispose of the Cybermen for you – without any more loss of life.'

'You deliberately told the Cybermen where you were, didn't you, Doctor? So you could make a deal with them.' She looked hard at him.

'They'd have found me sooner or later,' the Doctor said quietly. 'And how many more people would have died along the way? How many weak, defenceless people would have been killed as they tore this city apart to find me? They need me in order to survive, and that's the thing that drives them. Not emotions, not love or hate or ambition or greed. Survival.'

'The Cybermen want you to reopen some gateway, bring back their army. Would you do that?'

'No.'

'Not even to save your friend?'

'No.'

'How can I be sure of that? How can I be sure you wouldn't sacrifice us all to save her life?'

'Because I *can't* do it,' said the Doctor. 'The gate they want me to open is closed forever. Even to me.'

'Then they'll kill you both.'

'Oh, I do wish you hadn't said that. Look, I've got a sort of a plan,' the Doctor told her. 'OK, it's not fully worked out, and a lot depends on luck. But, for it to work, I have to be in the Dome with the Cybermen – and with the TARDIS.'

She studied him a moment longer. 'All right. But we'll attack the Dome and destroy the remaining Cybermen anyway. If you want to be in there when we do... This way, Doctor.'

They walked back towards the now floodlit parade ground, where squads of soldiers and medics were clearing away the debris of battle and carrying off the dead and wounded. On the far side of the parade ground, the main gates were open. A convoy of army trucks was driving through them.

'The assault force is arriving,' Sheila said with satisfaction. 'I'd better brief them. This way.'

She led him to the concrete archway, guarded by saluting sentries, that formed the entrance to the vault, and punched a security code into the electronic lock. Massive steel doors slid slowly back, and they moved into a concrete corridor ending in a lift, guarded by yet more soldiers.

The lift took them down to a vast chamber, lined with steel and reinforced concrete. It was packed with workbenches, lab compartments and crates of supplies and equipment. And there, in a dark alcove, stood the TARDIS. The Doctor beamed and patted it affectionately.

'I'll detail a squad of men to get it back to the surface for you,' offered Sheila.

'No, no,' said the Doctor hastily. 'I'll take care of all that. You've got a lot to do. Your assault force is waiting.'

'If you're sure... Goodbye, Doctor, and good luck.'

'I'll see you at the Dome,' said the Doctor, and disappeared into the TARDIS.

Sheila Sarandon shrugged and turned away.

Inside the TARDIS the Doctor stood over the control console, thinking furiously. He had to get this exactly right. Strange that a simple journey of just a few miles should be so much harder than a trip to Mars or the moon.

His fingers moved carefully over the controls.

Captain Sarandon had almost reached the corridor that led to the lift when she heard a strange sound. It was a sort of wheezing – yet there seemed to be a kind of groaning as well.

She turned and was just in time to see the battered old police box fade away. She shook her head – disappearing Cybermen, disappearing police boxes...

Dismissing them from her mind, Sheila

headed towards the assault force. Whoever was supposed to be in command, she knew who was really going to be running things...

CHAPTER FIFTEEN

ARRIVAL

MARTHA STOOD IN THE vast and shadowy Dome, considering her next move.

There were only two Cybermen with her now. The trouble was, the Cyberman told to guard her stayed close to her side at all times. Martha was sure that it would grab her at once if she tried to escape. Even if she managed to dodge away from him, it could easily shoot her down before she got far.

The other Cyberman was busily working on the complex electronic equipment. It seemed to be receiving signals of some kind.

Then the air shimmered and another Cyberman appeared.

It stood for a moment, gazing almost arrogantly around. Somehow Martha sensed that this was the Cyberleader. She waited, but no other Cybermen appeared – and there was no sign of the Doctor.

'The attack squad was destroyed,' the

Cyberleader told the two Cybermen. 'The humans have improved their weapons.'

'We have lost the entire attack squad. We have no more in reserve,' said one.

Was there reproach in the Cyberman's voice? Perhaps it was a rival for the position of leader, Martha thought. If Cybermen felt any emotion, it would surely be the lust for power. And perhaps these Cybermen, so recently human and converted quickly during the invasion, had a little more humanity than they should?

'The loss is of no importance,' said the Cyberleader. 'Soon our army will return from the Void.'

'That is impossible. You have failed in your mission. You have not captured the Doctor.'

'It is not necessary to capture the Doctor. He knows that this human is our prisoner. To save her life, he will come here of his own accord.'

'Will you free the Doctor and the human if he helps us?'

'No. The Doctor is a dangerous enemy. We shall kill them both.'

The sheer injustice of it made Martha angry. 'That's not fair. You promised to let us go if the Doctor helped you.'

'Promises made to inferior species have no meaning.'

'I'll show you who's inferior,' Martha muttered.

The Cyberman guarding her said, 'What if the Doctor does not come?'

'He *will* come.'

The worst thing about it, thought Martha, was that the Cyberleader was quite right. If there was any chance of freeing her, the Doctor would come. He'd come if there was no chance at all.

Sure enough, a familiar sound filled the air, and the TARDIS appeared beside the collection of Cyber-equipment. The door opened, and the Doctor stepped out, leaving the door open behind him. He looked round happily.

'Oh, that's brilliant! An inspired piece of navigation, if I say so myself. These very short trips are the hardest, you know. Hello Martha. You all right?'

'Never better,' said Martha. 'I've been having a lovely time. Song and dance and great conversation.'

The Doctor seemed not to notice her sarcasm. 'Good, good. Glad you're happy.' He looked around him. 'Wonderful place, the Dome. Of course, it's not really a proper dome at all. Not self-supporting, you see. Properly speaking, it's a mast-supported, dome-shaped cable network.

Did you know it's covered with coated glass-fibre fabric...'

'You must begin your task, Doctor,' said the Cyberleader impatiently. 'There is much to do. Unless you succeed—'

'Don't bother with the usual threats,' said the Doctor wearily. 'If I don't open the gateway to the Void for your Cyber-army, you'll kill Martha – and me as well.'

'That is correct. The Cybermen will return.'

'There you are again,' the Doctor said. 'Millennium Dome – not a proper dome. Cybermen – not proper men.'

'You're not really going to help them, Doctor?' Martha said in surprise.

'Oh, I'm afraid I have to, Martha. There's simply no other way. I mean, what else can I do? Stand here and watch you die? Not a lot of fun in that, is there?'

'But you said you—'

Hastily, the Doctor interrupted her. 'I know what I said, Martha. I said I *wouldn't* do it. I said I *wouldn't* do it whatever happened. But things have changed.'

He hadn't said that at all, thought Martha. He'd said he *couldn't* – that it was impossible. But 'couldn't' was clearly a word he didn't want the Cybermen to hear.

She made a last attempt to warn him. 'They're going to kill us both anyway, even if you do help them.'

'Now, now, Martha,' said the Doctor infuriatingly. 'The Cybermen are an honourable race, I'm sure they'd never break their word.'

'And if you believe that, you'll believe anything,' said Martha quietly. But obviously the Doctor didn't believe it at all. He was up to something.

Quickly, Martha reviewed the situation. Things were already improving. They were together in the Dome, and they were close to the open door of the TARDIS. Once inside, they'd be safe. She decided to watch and wait.

The Doctor moved over to the equipment complex and studied it. 'Another fine mess,' he said scornfully. 'Where did you collect this load of rubbish? Fell of the back of a lorry, did it?'

The Cyberleader took the question literally. 'It has not fallen. Some is our own Cyber-equipment, which we retrieved from the Torchwood Tower. The rest we took from the humans.'

The Doctor continued his examination. 'Well I can tell you now, most of it's no use at all. I mean, who sold you that bit, then?' He paused. 'Except, perhaps...' He leant forwards, examining the teleportation equipment. 'This might just possibly...'

The Doctor straightened up, addressing the Cyberleader. 'I think I can boost the power of the teleportation equipment so that it reaches clear into the Void. That will create the gateway you want. Yes, that's the way.' He nodded at the Cybermen, hoping they wouldn't realise what nonsense he was talking. 'Mind you, I shall have to link it up to the TARDIS console – it's the only way to boost the power.'

'Power is available here.'

'Not enough, not nearly enough. You don't use hamsters, by the way, do you?' He waved the question aside. 'Never mind, not important. Now, I'll need heavy-duty cables, lots of them. It's a big job and we haven't got much time. I suppose you realise that the Army is on its way here to attack you?'

'They will not succeed,' said the Cyberleader. He pointed to a complex piece of equipment, standing aside from the rest. It was throbbing with power. 'We have established a force field around the Dome.'

'Let's hope it holds,' said the Doctor, shooting Martha a meaningful look. 'I'd hate for that to go wrong or get damaged or anything. Right then, let's get started.'

'We will assist you.' The Cyberleader turned to the third Cyberman. 'You will continue to guard the girl. At the first sign of treachery – kill her!'

CHAPTER SIXTEEN

THE GATEWAY OPENS

THE ASSAULT FORCE COMMAND truck was parked outside the main gates of the Millennium Dome. Floodlights lit the whole area. Captain Sarandon stood beside the truck, waiting impatiently. Beside her was Colonel Barnard, a small terrier-like man with a bristling white moustache. He had fought the Cybermen, although not very successfully, during the invasion. He was itching for another chance at them.

'How much longer?' he snarled.

'Best to secure the perimeter, sir,' said Sheila Sarandon smoothly. 'We don't want to lose them now.'

A tall young lieutenant ran up and saluted. 'Perimeter secured, sir.'

'Good,' snapped Colonel Barnard. 'Order general advance.'

'Can't sir,' said the lieutenant.

'What do you mean, "can't"?'

'We can't move forward sir, not at any point

of the perimeter. There's some kind of force field around the whole place. It pushes back men and vehicles.'

'Then break through it.'

'The technical blokes are working on it now sir. They're sending for some new kind of explosive. They say it'll take a really massive explosion – big enough to destroy the whole place.'

'Good riddance,' said Colonel Barnard. 'Damn place was never any use anyway.'

A bit hard on the Doctor, if he was in there, not to mention his companion, thought Sheila. Still, sacrifices had to be made in war.

'Right,' said the Doctor. 'That's it. Stand back everybody.'

A spider's web of power cables ran from the TARDIS console and through the open door. They connected the console to the teleportation equipment.

'I'll just go into the TARDIS and power it all up,' said the Doctor. 'The gateway to the Void will appear at the teleportation point. Your fellow Cybermen will know it's opening and very soon they'll start coming through.' The Doctor headed for the open TARDIS door, stepping over the cables.

'We still have your associate,' warned the Cyberleader. 'You will leave the TARDIS once the power is on.'

'Oh, don't worry,' said the Doctor. 'I wouldn't miss this for worlds.'

He entered the TARDIS, went to the console and pulled a huge lever. The teleportation equipment began throbbing with power. The Doctor emerged and stood waiting with the Cybermen.

For a moment, nothing happened. Then, slowly, a glowing portal appeared in the air. It was the size and shape of the TARDIS door. Faint and shadowy at first, it grew larger, brighter... Soon it was huge and cavernous. Pale blue light blazed from inside.

The Cybermen stared at it with what looked like awe – even the one guarding Martha. Seizing her chance, she leaped away, dashed to the force-field generator and kicked it, again and again. It fizzed and crackled, and Martha yanked out a cable from the side, sending off a shower of sparks. Her Cyberman guard raised its arm and fired. Martha threw herself sideways – just in time. The energy blast missed her and struck the force-field generator. It exploded into flame. She scrambled to her feet and ducked behind a crate.

The Cyber-engineer turned from the glowing doorway and studied the energy readings on the teleportation dials. 'We have been cheated,' it decided. 'This gateway does not lead to the Void.'

The Cyberleader trained his wrist-gun on the Doctor. 'Where does the gateway lead?'

'It leads to the Void, I tell you,' shouted the Doctor. 'Your readings won't be accurate, will they? You're trying to get a reading from nothing. That's what "void" means.' He turned towards the glowing gateway and pointed. 'Look, they're coming through!'

Something was indeed coming through the gateway, but it wasn't a Cyberman. It was a colossal head, jaws full of sharp teeth, snapping and biting at the air as the massive creature tried to force its way through the opening. A Tyrannosaurus Rex.

The Cyber-engineer fired at it, and the energy-blast hammered into the dinosaur's head. It gave a tremendous roar of rage, and lunged towards the Cyber-engineer. Huge jaws closed round the Cyberman, ripping off its head. The second Cyberman fired, but again to no effect. Enraged, the giant T-Rex snatched the Cyberman and dragged its thrashing body back through the glowing gateway.

'You have betrayed us Doctor!' cried the Cyberleader.

He raised his weapon and fired. But the Doctor ducked beneath the blast. In a single, rapid movement, he wrenched free the main power cable and thrust it into the Cyberleader's chest.

There was a fierce crackle of power, and sparks flowed around the Cyberleader's body. His eyes glowed red and smoke poured from his mouth. Spinning round, he crashed to the ground.

Martha slowly emerged from behind her crate. 'Well done, Doctor.'

She turned to look at the glowing gateway and saw that it had disappeared. It had vanished when the Doctor disconnected the power cable.

'Where did that thing come from?'

The Doctor had freed the other end of the power cable from the TARDIS console and dragged it clear. Now he was unplugging the rest of the cables and hurling them out of the door.

'Just a simple space-time portal,' he said. 'Used to muck about with them at school. I connected their teleportation set-up to the TARDIS at the exact point in space and time where we last landed. You remember our little field trip? Tommy T-Rex lunges at the TARDIS and, at the same moment we left, the gateway opened and let him get the Cybermen. Doctor dix points, Team Cyberman nul points.'

'What'll happen to the Cyberman the creature dragged off?'

'I imagine it must be pretty hard to digest. The T-Rex will probably drop bits of it all round the Jurassic period.' He grinned. 'Got to keep the archaeologists guessing.'

The Doctor freed the last cable and went to the TARDIS door. 'Come on, Martha, time we were out of here.'

'Not so fast, Doctor,' called a familiar voice. 'Surely you're not leaving without saying goodbye?'

Captain Sheila Sarandon came running into the Dome, armed soldiers behind her. Confused and cautious, the soldiers covered the Doctor and Martha with their rifles.

'Ah, there you are,' said the Doctor. 'Glad you could join us at last.' He pointed to the giant silver shape on the ground. 'And there's the last Cyberman on Earth for you, stone-cold dead. You can have it stuffed and put it in the Mess. Or melt it down for regimental silver.'

Sheila Sarandon looked thoughtfully at him. 'My superiors are very interested in you,

Doctor. They want you arrested and shipped off to them.'

The Doctor sighed. 'You're not going to be difficult are you? I do hope you're not going to be difficult. We've had enough unpleasantness for one day already, and I much prefer being pleasant. Don't you?' He smiled.

Sheila smiled too. She was expecting a promotion out of all this, and she was in a very good mood. 'All right, Doctor, we owe you this one. Off you go. But don't hurry back!'

'Well, of all the ingratitude,' said Martha indignantly.

The Doctor grinned and blew Sheila a kiss, then pulled Martha inside the TARDIS. The door closed behind them.

Sheila Sarandon turned to her soldiers. 'Watch closely. You're not going to believe this.'

With a strange, wheezing, groaning sound, the TARDIS faded away.

Inside, the Doctor adjusted controls and checked read-outs. Martha was emotionally shattered and completely exhausted. The Doctor, on the other hand, seemed quite unaffected by their recent adventures.

'Where now then – and when?' he asked, flexing his fingers ready to set a new course.

Martha sighed and leaned against the console. 'I don't know, Doctor. Somewhere nice and peaceful. You choose.'

The Doctor beamed. 'I know just the place!'

His hands moved over the controls.

READ ON THE BEACH!
Win a holiday to Barbados

Fly to the beautiful four-star **Amaryllis Beach Resort** set on a white, sandy beach on the south coast of Barbados.

For more information about the resort please visit www.amaryllisbeachresort.com. letsgo2.com
Holidays created by you...

Other prizes to be won

- **£100-worth of books for all the family**
  (we have five sets to give away)
- **A limousine for an evening in London**
- **£100-worth of M&S vouchers**
  (we have two sets to give away)

HOW TO ENTER
Fill in the form below.
Name two authors who have written Quick Reads books:

1. _____

2. _____

Your name: _____

Address: _____

_____

Telephone number: _____

Tell us where you heard about Quick Reads: _____

_____

☐ **I have read and agree to the terms and conditions
  on the back of this page**

Send this form to: Quick Reads Competition, Colman Getty, 28 Windmill Street, London, W1T 2JJ or enter the competition on our website www.quickreads.org.uk.
Closing date: 1 September 2007

QUICK READS COMPETITION

TERMS AND CONDITIONS

1. You must be aged 18 years or older and resident in the UK to enter this competition. If you or an immediate family member works or is otherwise involved in the Quick Reads initiative or in this promotion, you may not enter.

2. To enter, fill in the entry form in the back of a Quick Reads book, in ink or ballpoint pen, tear it out and send it to: Quick Reads Competition, Colman Getty, 28 Windmill Street, London W1T 2JJ before the closing date of 1 September 2007. Or enter on our website at www.quickreads.org.uk before 1 September 2007.

3. You may enter as many times as you wish. Each entry must be on a separate form found in the back of a Quick Reads book or a separate entry on the www.quickreads.org.uk website. No entries will be returned.

4. By entering this competition you agree to the terms and conditions.

5. We cannot be responsible for entry forms lost, delayed or damaged in the post. Proof of posting is not accepted as proof of delivery.

6. The prizes will be awarded to the people who have answered the competition questions correctly and whose entry forms are drawn out first, randomly, by an independent judge after the closing date. We will contact the winners by telephone by 1 November 2007.

7. There are several prizes:
   First Prize (there will be one first prize-winner) – Seven nights' stay at a four-star resort in Barbados. The holiday is based on two people sharing a self-catering studio room with double or twin beds and includes: return flights from a London airport, seven nights' accommodation (excludes meals), use of the resort gym and non-motorised water sports. Travel to and from the London airport is not included. You will be responsible for airport transfers, visa, passport and insurance requirements, vaccinations (if applicable), passenger taxes, charges, fees and surcharges (the amount of which is subject to change). You must travel before 1 May 2008. You must book at least four weeks before departure and bookings will be strictly subject to availability. The prize-winner will be bound by the conditions of booking issued by the operator.
   Second Prize (there will be five second prize-winners) – A set of books selected by the competition Promoter including books suitable for men, women and children – to be provided by Quick Reads up to the retail value of £100.
   Third Prize (there will be one third prize-winner) – An evening in a limousine travelling around London between the hours of 6 p.m. and midnight in a limousine provided by us. You and up to five other people will be collected from any one central London point and can travel anywhere within inner London. Champagne is included. Travel to and from London is not included.
   Fourth Prize (there will be two fourth prize-winners) – £100-worth of Marks & Spencer vouchers to be spent in any branch of M&S.

8. There is no cash alternative for any of these prizes and unless agreed otherwise in writing the prizes are non-refundable and non-transferable.

9. The Promoter reserves the right to vary, amend, suspend or withdraw any or all of the prizes if this becomes necessary for reasons beyond its control.

10. The names and photographs of prize-winners may be used for publicity by the Promoter, provided they agree at the time.

11. Details of prize-winners' names and counties will be available for one month after the close of the promotion by writing to the Promoter at the address set out below.

12. The Promoter, its associated companies and agents, exclude responsibility for any act or failure by any third-party supplier, including airlines, hotels or travel companies, as long as this is within the law. Therefore this does not apply to personal injury or negligence.

13. The Promoter is Quick Reads/World Book Day Limited, 272 Vauxhall Bridge Road, London SW1V 1BA.

Quick Reads
Pick up a book today

Quick Reads are published alongside and in partnership with BBC RaW.

We would like to thank all our partners in the Quick Reads project for their help and support:

NIACE
unionlearn
National Book Tokens
The Vital Link
The Reading Agency
National Literacy Trust
Booktrust
Welsh Books Council
The Basic Skills Agency, Wales
Accent Press
Communities Scotland

Quick Reads would also like to thank the Department for Education and Skills, Arts Council England and World Book Day for their sponsorship, and NIACE (the National Institute for Adult Continuing Education) for their outreach work.

Quick Reads is a World Book Day initiative.

Quick Reads

Books in the Quick Reads series

New titles

A Dream Come True	Maureen Lee
Burning Ambition	Allen Carr
Lily	Adèle Geras
Made of Steel	Terrance Dicks
Reading My Arse	Ricky Tomlinson
The Sun Book of Short Stories	
Survive the Worst and Aim for the Best	Kerry Katona
Twenty Tales from the War Zone	John Simpson

Backlist

Blackwater	Conn Iggulden
Book Boy	Joanna Trollope
Chickenfeed	Minette Walters
Cleanskin	Val McDermid
Danny Wallace and the Centre of the Universe	Danny Wallace
Don't Make Me Laugh	Patrick Augustus
The Grey Man	Andy McNab
Hell Island	Matthew Reilly
How to Change Your Life in Seven Steps	John Bird
I Am a Dalek	Gareth Roberts
The Name You Once Gave Me	Mike Phillips
Star Sullivan	Maeve Binchy

Don't get by get on 0800 100 900

We provide courses for anyone who wants to develop their skills. All courses are free and are available in your local area. If you'd like to find out more, phone 0800 100 900.

First Choice Books

If you enjoyed this Quick Reads book, you'll find more great reads on www.firstchoicebooks.org.uk or at your local library.

First Choice is part of The Vital Link, promoting reading for pleasure. To find out more about The Vital Link visit www.vitallink.org.uk.

Find out what the BBC's RaW (Reading and Writing Campaign) has to offer at www.bbc.co.uk/raw.

Quick Reads

I Am a Dalek
by Gareth Roberts

BBC Books

Equipped with space suits, golf clubs and a flag, the Doctor and Rose are planning to live it up on the Moon, Apollo-mission style. But the TARDIS has other plans, landing them instead in a village on the south coast of England; a picture-postcard sort of place where nothing much happens...until now.

Archaeologists have dug up a Roman mosaic, dating from the year 70 AD. It shows scenes from ancient myths, bunches of grapes – and a Dalek. A few days later a young woman, rushing to get to work, is knocked over and killed by a bus. Then she comes back to life.

It's not long before all hell breaks loose, and the Doctor and Rose must use all their courage and cunning against an alien enemy – and a not-quite-alien accomplice – who are intent on destroying humanity.

Featuring the Doctor and Rose as played by David Tennant and Billie Piper in the hit series from BBC Television.